Беларусь

To Raif Badawi, his wife Eusaf Haidar
and their children Tirad, Najwa and Miriyam.

Jacques goldstyn

Letters to a
Prisoner

Jacques goldstyn

Owlkids Books

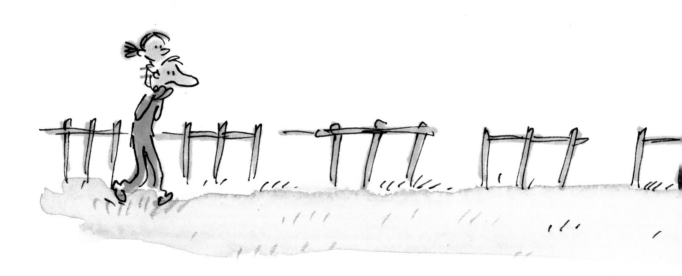

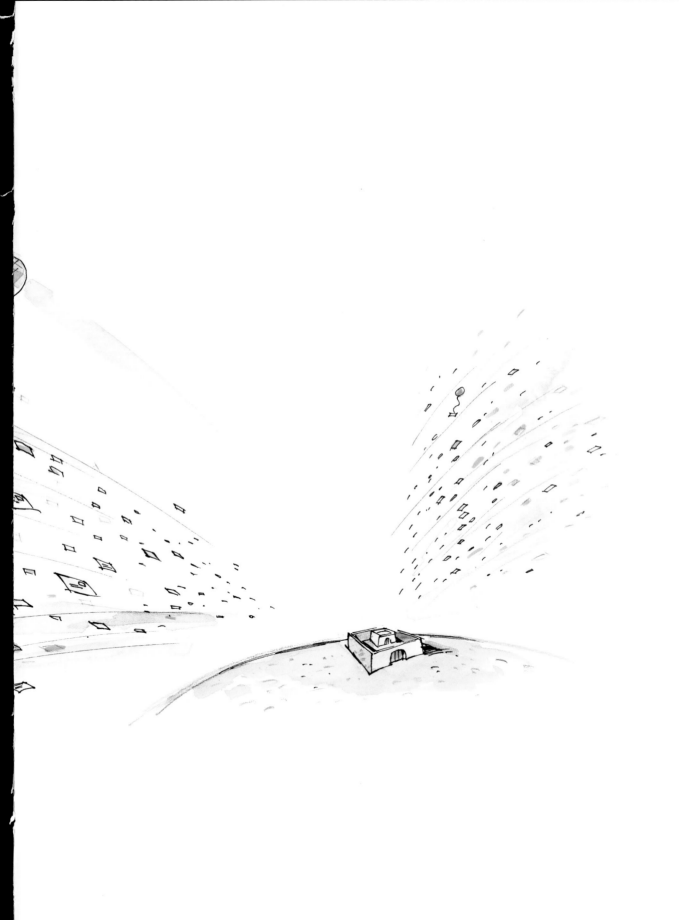

The first time I took part in Amnesty International's Write for Rights letter-writing marathon, all sorts of people were involved—from the young and old to the famous and not-so famous.

Despite our differences, we all had one thing in common: the desire to write to a person who had been unjustly imprisoned for his or her ideas.

To inspire us and our messages of support, Amnesty International (a human rights organization) provided us with photos of the prisoners, as well as information about them. It helped our letter writing to know why these people had been imprisoned.

It made me happy to know our letters and drawings had a chance of reaching these prisoners. Better still, our show of solidarity might help these wrongly imprisoned people reclaim their freedom.

My letter writing inspired me to write this story.

And perhaps this story will inspire you. Each year, letter-writing campaigns are held in cities all over the world. Last year, cards, letters, and emails were sent from over 185 countries. If you're interested in supporting this cause and making a difference, you can join Amnesty International's efforts by participating in a Write for Rights event or by organizing one in your community.

Jacques goldstyn

Text and illustrations © 2015 Jacques Goldstyn
Translation © 2017 Owlkids Books Inc.; Translated by Angela Keenlyside

This edition published in 2017 by Owlkids Books Inc.

Published under the title *Le prisonnier sans frontières* in 2015 by Bayard Canada Livres Inc.

Owlkids Books acknowledges the financial support of the Canada Council for the Arts, the Ontario Arts Council, the Government of Canada through the Canada Book Fund (CBF) and the Government of Ontario through the Ontario Media Development Corporation's Book Initiative for our publishing activities.

Published in Canada by
Owlkids Books Inc.
10 Lower Spadina Avenue
Toronto, ON M5V 2Z2

Published in the United States by
Owlkids Books Inc.
1700 Fourth Street
Berkeley, CA 94710

Library and Archives Canada Cataloguing in Publication

Goldstyn, Jacques [Prisonnier sans frontières. English]
     Letters to a prisoner / written and illustrated by Jacques Goldstyn; translated by Angela Keenlyside.

Translation of: Le prisonnier sans frontières.

ISBN 978-1-77147-251-7 (hardcover)

     1. Stories without words. 2. Graphic novels. I. Keenlyside, Angela, translator II. Title.
III. Title: Prisonnier sans frontières. English.

PN6733.G64P7513 2017   j741.5'971   C2017-900007-1

Library of Congress Control Number: 2016962524

English edition designed by: Danielle Arbour

Manufactured in Dongguan, China, in April 2017, by Toppan Leefung Packaging & Printing (Dongguan) Co., Ltd.
Job #BAYDC40

A   B   C   D   E   F

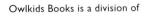

Publisher of Chirp, chickaDEE and OWL
www.owlkidsbooks.com

Owlkids Books is a division of Bayard CANADA